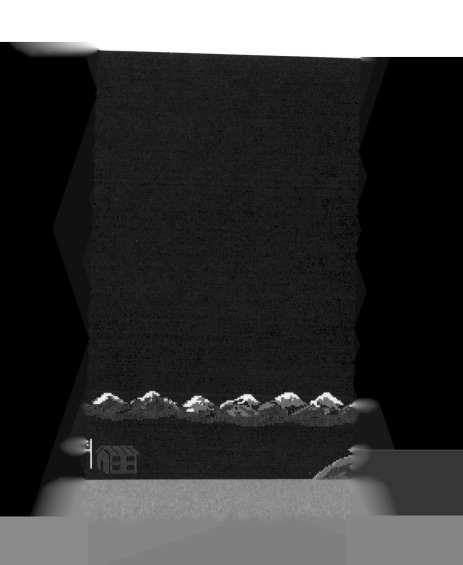

The Oregon Trail™

hmhbooks.com

The text was set in Garamond.
The display text was set in Pixel-Western, Press Start 2P, and Slim Thin Pixelettes.
Illustrations by Gustavo Viselner

Library of Congress Cataloging-in-Publication Data is available.

ISBN: 978-1-328-62716-2 paper over board
ISBN: 978-1-328-62717-9 paperback

Printed in the United States of America
DOC 10 9 8 7 6 5 4 3 2 1
4500751511

The Oregon Trail™

ALONE IN
THE WILD

by
JESSE WILEY

Houghton Mifflin Harcourt
BOSTON   NEW YORK

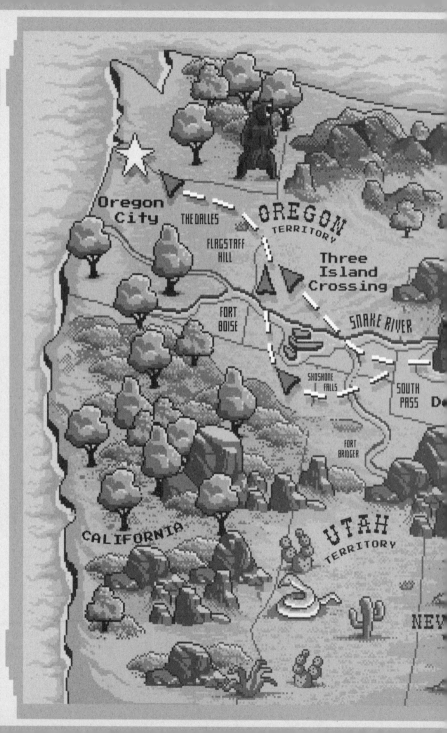

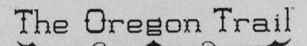

The Oregon Trail

UNORGANIZED TERRITORY

MINNESOTA TERRITORY

Chimney Rock

SCOTTS BLUFF

IOWA

COURTHOUSE ROCK and JAIL ROCK

FORT KEARNY

Independence, MISSOURI

XICO

TEXAS

★

A Guide through Territories to the North and West

South Pass, Wyoming
JUNE 19, 1849

The Oregon Trail™

The Journey West

It's 1849, and you and your family are settlers on the journey of a lifetime on the Oregon Trail. So far, the trip has been filled with challenges: runaway oxen, bandits, illness, dangerous wildlife, broken wagon parts, and more. You're lucky you've all made it to South Pass, Wyoming—your halfway point.

As you continue on your trek West, you'll face even more dangers such as starvation, sickness, frostbite, and bad weather. It will take all your grit and smarts to make it to your destination—Oregon City.

Beware! Only one path will get you there safely.

There are twenty possible endings, full of challenges, twists and turns, and incredible discoveries.

You come across a hungry pack of wolves—what do you do?

You're lost alone in the woods—how do you survive?

Look out! Avalanche! Where can you go?

Your choices might send you somewhere unexpected or land you in harmful situations. Or even worse—you might not survive the journey!

Be prepared! Before you start, be sure to read the Guide to the Trail on page 148. It will help you survive in the wilderness and make better decisions.

Along the Trail, you might run into other travelers, guides, or Native American peoples such as the Shoshone and Tenino Nations, who may provide advice, assistance, and friendship. At other times, you'll have to trust your gut to make the right decisions.

It's up to you!
What will you choose?

→ **Ready?** ←

LET'S FORGE A PATH TO

OREGON CITY!

You have more than 1,000 miles until you reach Oregon City—or at least that's what you think. Your wagon train captain, Buck Sanders, lost your only map about a month ago when he discarded supplies from the wagons to lighten their load.

Since Buck lost the map, you've all been relying on the kindness of strangers, trail guides, and the position of the sun to find your way West. The oxen in your ten-wagon train are getting more exhausted by the minute on a trail lined with cast-iron skillets and extra wagon parts. Luckily, you've stayed calm and stuck to the Trail.

Today, your wagon is corralled by Little Wind River. Clear skies and sunshine have you and your wagon train in great spirits.

Mama yells over to you. "We're going to ford that river soon. Let's caulk our wagon before sundown."

"Anne," Pa calls to Mama. "Don't

work our sweet child too hard—
I'll need help preparing our
meal soon."

"Well, well, well." Buck
Sanders approaches your
wagon. His overgrown handlebar
mustache covers his mouth.
"I see the Winters family is doin' especially well
today. I am goin' 'round and tellin' folks that we will
camp here tonight, get some rest, and get movin'
first thing in the morn'. And, uh, please keep an eye
on that dog of yours. He's gettin' into other people's
business."

"Snap!" You whistle to your lovable dog. "Here,
boy!"

"Buck"—Mama's face screws up—
"the sky is clear and the weather is great.
Let's cross the Little Wind River today.
We're working hard to get all of the
wagons caulked and we still have five
hours of sunlight left in the day."

"Anne." Buck smiles and tugs on his mustache. "The other folks are exhausted. Not as strong as y'all three, I guess." Buck whistles to the larger wagon train. "Let's get these wagons circled up!"

As Buck walks away, Mama takes Pa aside. "John, I knew we couldn't trust Buck as wagon train captain. He has no experience, and I can't believe he lost the map—the only map we had!"

Pa calms Mama. "There's nothing we can do now, Anne, save for peeling off from the group, which is not smart or safe. Let's just get our chores done and rest up for tomorrow so we're fresh for the river crossing."

Mama gives him a hug and then you both help Pa finish making dinner—a ration of bacon and steamed dandelions with fresh venison. You're thankful Pa hunted a deer last night. Supplies are running lower than predicted, so your family is

measuring out food—it's got to last for the rest of your trip. Stopping at general stores and trading posts are viable options, but not always available, and you don't have a lot of money with you. Plus, with an unreliable wagon train captain and no map, who knows if you'll pass any of the trading posts or forts. You've all worked hard to gather a lot of berries and various edible plants along the way while other folks in your wagon train have been more successful in hunting deer and rabbits. They've shared with you so far, but there's no guarantee that their generosity will continue.

Rest up, the next leg of the journey is a calamity!

★ ★ ★

You wake to a loud whistle and a crack of thunder.

Buck Sanders is running around your corral circle in a frenzy. "We gotta go now! 'Fore the river swells too high, ya hear?"

"In the middle of the night, Buck?" Pa protests. "It's not even midnight. The fire embers are still smoldering from when I put it out two hours ago."

"Now is the time!" Buck yells as the sky starts to spit. "The clouds are rollin' in against the moon. We've gotta move!"

Your family could stay behind, but without a map and the protection of a wagon train, you'd have no chance. You follow everyone and roll into the dark.

Your wagon is last to launch into the river. "It floats!" you yell to Mama. She smiles by the lantern light, proud of your good work. Snap sits next to her, anxiously whimpering.

Lightning strikes!

Torrential rain pours out of the sky and floods the river. Wild rapids develop over rocks. Your wagon isn't built for this.

You paddle faster with handmade oars you've carved from broken tree branches. You knew they'd come in handy.

When you're halfway across the river, fear fills Mama's face. Then it happens. In a flash, you are tossed into the rushing black water.

"Overboard!" she screams to Pa, but he is almost across the river, leading the oxen.

Ice-cold water shocks you. It fills your mouth
as you bob up and down. Swimming against the
powerful river current is nearly impossible in your
drenched, heavy clothes. Your arm muscles tire
against the force of the water. You muster up as much
strength as you can and grab a wagon wheel spoke,
but your grip weakens. You scream to Mama as she
holds her hand out. But just as you reach toward her,
river water washes over you. Snap yelps and falls into
the careening waves. The current is stronger than
your grip on the wagon wheel. It takes you under.

You wake coughing up water on the riverbank. You look around. The sun is peeking through the trees in the west. You see no wagons, no animals—no Snap— no one around you. No Mama. No Pa.

You're alone. You have no support and no food, and you are lost. You were half awake when your family got the call to ford the river—with only seconds to throw on your clothes and slip a few things into your pockets. How far downriver did the water carry you? There is no one around for miles and miles. There's no time to waste. You'll have to use your survival skills to find your wagon train as soon as possible.

Your head pounds. Thunder rumbles in the gray clouds. As you slowly stand up, dirt and leaves fall off your wet clothes.

Panic takes over you for a split second. But panicking isn't an option.

You wipe your face and look around. No family. No wagons. No oxen. No one and nothing in sight. Judging by the light, it's mid-to-late afternoon, though it's hard to tell with the overcast weather. You sit down on a flat rock and try to piece together what happened.

The storm. Mama. The river. It all comes back to you. You remember you're close to South Pass, Wyoming—the easiest way to cross through the treacherous Rocky Mountains. Then, you remember Snap. You hope everyone made it out of the river.

"Mama!" You put your hands to your mouth. "Snap! Mama! Pa! Where are you? Can anybody

hear me?" Your hoarse voice is weak. In the distance, lightning charges the sky. Another storm.

You shiver and wrap your arms around yourself. Your hair and clothes are still damp. You need to find dry clothes—and your family.

"Hello? Hello, can anyone hear me?" You hear the echo of your own voice.

No response.

You swallow. Your throat is sore. *Stay calm.* You hope camp is close. Your stomach grumbles.

You spot a few dandelions nearby. You know from listening to one of your wagon train guides that in the most dire of circumstances, the flowers can be eaten. You pick several dandelions and stuff them into your mouth. They're nutty and bitter in flavor and taste better than you expected.

You have to keep moving.

You start walking, calling for Mama, for Snap, every few minutes. You follow the rushing river upstream, stepping through bushes. The mud pushes through your soaked boots, making every step heavier and heavier. You hope you're going the right way.

After you've followed the river for an hour or two, nothing looks familiar.

A loud boom of thunder startles you. You bite your lip and brace yourself. If you can't find your wagon train, you'll have to start looking for shelter. It's getting dark.

Your hope wanes, but then you see something familiar: an oddly shaped rock in the distance, Lizard

Head Peak. It was your wagon train's North Star on the trek here. You recognize the surrounding area. Your spirits lift, and despite your exhausted body, you pick up your feet and break into a slow jog. You're so close—you have a good feeling.

"Pa? Mama? Snap! I'm here! I'm all right!"

Faster and faster you weave your way through the brush along the riverbank and down into the nook where your wagon train had set up camp before crossing the river. You finally push through a thick grove of trees, step out into the clearing, and look to the other side of the river.

No one.

Nothing.

No evidence of your wagon train or your family. They're *gone*.

You blink, not believing your eyes. In a daze, you stumble, staring at the blackened circle of rocks and ash that once was your campfire.

You scan the horizon, your heart pounding rapidly. You can't even find footprints or wheel ruts in the mud. The heavy rains have washed away any trace of your wagon train.

You feel a new rush of panic. You have no idea if your family made it across the wild river or if they, too, were swept down the river like you.

 An owl hoots nearby, and you jump. Darkness settles in. Should you continue to search for your wagon train, or set up your own camp and make a fire?

To search for your wagon train, turn to page 115

To make a fire, turn to page 138

You decide to put your limbs closer to the fire. You want to listen to Tatsa, but you're so cold that you can hardly breathe. More than that, you can't contain your growing panic about your numb hands and feet. You need to know that they will regain feeling—and soon. A little warmth couldn't hurt.

You inch closer to the fire and stick your hands and feet near the edge of the flames. Minutes pass. To your alarm, nothing happens. Your shaking has gotten worse. You wiggle even closer. A gust whips the fire toward you, igniting your feet in a spreading flame. You shriek and stamp out the flames, but your feet have been badly burned.

You never make it out of these snowy mountains.

☞ **THE END**

You decide to get to higher ground. You won't be near the river, but maybe if you climb high enough, you'll be able to get a better vantage point and maybe even spot a flag flying above Fort Hall in the distance. Lizard Head Peak is no longer in sight. You're not sure how far you've traveled in these mountains, but you know that you have a long way to go.

With Snap trotting at your side, you begin trekking to higher ground. The terrain grows rockier and steeper by the minute. You have to stop constantly to let Snap catch up to you, or carry him yourself. It's a more treacherous route than you'd anticipated—you almost slip and fall several times.

As the afternoon wears on into evening, you

try to find your way around the sharper cliffs and steeper inclines. Finally you reach a tall boulder, wipe your brow, and look around. You see nothing but mountains for miles and miles. What's worse, it looks like the path to the northwest—the way you need to travel—only gets more challenging.

You plop down onto the boulder, watching the sun sink into the mountains. You have to keep going.

"C'mon, Snap." You slide off the boulder and start toward a patch of trees to build a shelter and rest for the night. You eat some of the dried rabbit meat left over from earlier, but there's hardly enough for both you and Snap.

The next morning, you come across a grassy

nook full of flowers you've never seen before. Maybe some of them are edible. It would be a huge risk—some plants are poisonous—but you know you need to eat. Should you try to eat the flowers, or keep looking?

To eat the flowers, turn to page **31**

To keep looking, turn to page **125**

It's better to keep the fire going all night. That way, you'll be warm until the morning, and it will ward off any predators. Your clothes are still drying by the fire. At this point, it's too dark to build a shelter to protect you from the elements.

Dizzy from exhaustion, you hurry to find several large sticks and add them one by one to the fire. When the flames are roaring and crackling, reaching up nearly three feet into the air, you curl up nearby. Finally, the heat wraps you up like a blanket.

Maybe someone will see the smoke from the fire and come to rescue you. You fall asleep, lulled by the sound of the crackling flames.

Minutes later, you burst awake, coughing violently. Smoke fills your lungs. You bolt upright. There's smoke in your eyes, making you tear up. Forest fire! Sparks from your campfire caught onto branches overhead, and now the landscape around you is burning.

You stumble through the smoke and flame-filled woods, ash and embers falling all around you. You can't breathe. You won't make it out of this forest, never mind getting all the way to Oregon City.

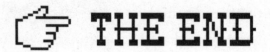 **THE END**

You run, but the wolves surround you, their fangs bared and gleaming, their ears curled back against their heads. They're twice as big as you are!

It's probably better to face the wolves down, to stare them in the eyes to show them you're not afraid. But as they draw closer, terror overwhelms you. You turn and bolt into the woods. You trip and scramble to pick yourself back up. You smell their stinky breath. One of them snaps at your ankles.

Just as all hope seems lost, you find a tall rock formation. You swing yourself up and climb onto the rocks, just as one wolf lunges for you. The wolves surround the rocks, growling, until they finally retreat into the woods.

You rest for a bit, but now you're exhausted—and parched. You spot a small stream only a few yards away, but you'll have to climb down to reach it. Hours pass. Finally, you decide you've waited long enough. You're certain that the wolves have gone on to find other prey.

Still casting a wary eye around the area, you make your way down off the rock formation and drop to the ground. You pause when you hear a twig snap in the distance, but you don't see anything but a bird flying away.

You hurry to the stream and kneel to drink. A shadow falls in front of you. The wolves have gotten you.

☞ THE END

You inspect the tiny bunches of flowers. It may be rock cress, a yellow or purple flower that grows in between boulders. You take off a tiny bud and eat it. It tastes surprisingly good—not bitter like dandelions. You try the white flowers next—they're delicious! After you eat as much as you can, you stuff a bunch of flowers into your pockets. They're not filling, but they do help ward off your immediate hunger pangs. Like the berries, they'll be handy in a pinch.

Snap watches you eat with round, doleful eyes.

You rub his belly and keep moving on. There has to be another rodent or rabbit he could catch.

As the breeze picks up, you smell something odd. Snap drops his nose to the ground and abruptly takes off, yelping. You follow him, startled.

"What is it, boy? Slow down!"

Huffing, you find him sniffing an animal lying on the ground. You grin, overwhelmed with relief.

"A deer! Good job, Snap!" As you draw closer, you recoil in disgust. The deer is dead and it's beginning to rot. Flies buzz around the half-eaten carcass.

You're briefly reminded of that last dinner you had the night before the big storm with Mama and Pa. You snap back to reality. Venison would fill your belly more than flowers. However, you could get really sick if you eat it. Should you cook it, or move on and find a better meal?

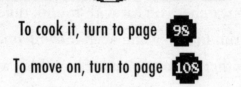

To cook it, turn to page 98

To move on, turn to page 108

Even though you've been lost on the prairie, you still hope that you can find your family with a little help from this wagon train.

"Thank you, but I think I need to try to find my parents."

Sam looks startled at your decision. "Well . . . all right. We don't have much food to spare, but we'll give you what we can."

In the end, they hand over only a small sack of cornmeal, some flour, salted buffalo meat, and stale johnnycakes. You say goodbye and watch the wagon train disappear over the horizon. You wonder if you've made a terrible mistake.

You spend several more days in the desolate prairie. The river has become a tiny, muddy stream. You have nothing to boil water in, so you have to drink directly from the stream. The water tastes weird.

One night, as you try to spark a flame with two sharp rocks, you hear footsteps.

"Hello?" You look up and see a dark shadow growing closer. "Who's there?"

You hear a gasp, and then someone calling your name.

"Mama? Pa? Is that you?"

Seconds later, you're enveloped in your parents' arms. The three of you have a joyful reunion. Pa lights a campfire and tells you that he and Mama had separated from your wagon train to search for you.

"We looked for you for days." Pa watches you devour a slab of bacon. He exchanges defeated looks with Mama. "Buck told us we had to move on. But Mama and I wouldn't have it. So we split from the wagon train to keep searching for you and left in a haste, we did. Had to drop most of our supplies. We're running on

bare bones. But that doesn't matter: we found you."

Your parents look exhausted and haggard, and they are low on food. Pa tries to hunt prairie dogs and vultures the next day, but he's only got one box of ammunition left. He's so tired that he misses most of his shots and wastes the bullets.

You and your parents may have found each other, but you're trekking across a harsh prairie with dwindling food and no support. You won't survive out here in the wild on your own for much longer.

 **THE END**

You trust Tatsa's instincts and decide to keep traveling with her. You turn to Smith's wagon train. "Thank you for the offer, but we'll continue on our own. We've found the Trail, we have our map, and we're almost to Oregon Territory now. I'm confident we'll be just fine."

William rubs his beard. "I don't think that's a great idea, but . . . if we can't take you along with us, we can at least spare some food and supplies for your travels ahead. This area's practically a desert. We've had a hard time of it ourselves."

"Thank you." You nod. "That would be very helpful."

Tatsa smiles warmly.

The travelers on Smith's wagon train cobble together some flour, bacon, and cornmeal for your journey. You can't carry much, but every little bit helps. The wagon train continues on. You, Tatsa, and Snap watch them disappear into the horizon.

Tatsa promptly turns away toward the river nearby. You follow.

With the Blue Mountains already in sight, you're relieved when you finally see green again after traversing through desert-like conditions along the Snake River. It's been at least two weeks. Rolling hills dotted with dark pines surround you as you pass over Crawford Hill for the Cascades and Mount Hood. The climb and descent through Crawford Hill is some of the most difficult terrain you've crossed, but you know it's easier on foot without heavy wagons. Your leg muscles ache.

Finally, your long descent gives way to flat plains as far as the eye can see. The map tells you the Columbia River is just north. You and Tatsa continue near the river due west until the Trail winds up into rolling green hills near The Dalles. After that, you head south into the pleasant, open Tygh Valley and start your journey into the Cascades. Snow-capped mountains covered with thick pine trees stretch up into the sky before you. You and Tatsa slowly climb up the unstable slope. The wind picks up. You shiver, huddling in your blanket. Patches of snow begin to appear on the Trail, and soon after, you find yourselves trudging through deep drifts.

"Come on. We should hunt for food before it gets dark." Tatsa pats you on the back. "The movement will get your body warm. Think of the nice, juicy elk meat!"

"Or the lean, tough elk meat." You slog through the snow after her.

"The only thing that's lean and tough up here is *me*," she teases.

"Hey!" You gather up a ball of snow and hurl it at her back. She shrieks and returns the favor. Snap, who's been eating snow and chasing squirrels every moment he can, bounces between the both of you.

Whumph!

A strange sound halts your fun. Thundering comes ominously closer and closer. You see it: piles of snow sliding down the mountainside, crashing through the pines, headed right for you. It's an avalanche! Should you try to outrun the fast-moving snow or climb a nearby tree?

To outrun it, turn to page **73**

To climb a tree, turn to page **135**

You stay in hiding and avoid the girl entirely. You're afraid you can't trust anyone but yourself. You've heard stories of mountain men prowling these hills, of pioneers being robbed by fur trappers and bandits.

Although Snap seems to want to run out and meet the girl, you hold him back. Cautiousness wins out in the end. You turn back up the mountain to try to make a wide angle around the girl.

When you think you might have passed her, you can't find the river. You continue downhill, hoping you'll eventually run into it again. But the longer you hike down, the steeper and rockier your decline becomes. You stop to check your location against the sun. Your heart sinks. You've gotten turned around

and you've been heading southeast—the opposite direction of where you need to go!

Your path only becomes more difficult. You traverse steep and unforgiving rocky terrain with sharp drops and overhanging cliffs that look out into the valley below. You wander for hours. Attempting to scale down the boulders, you wait for Snap to follow after you.

Then you hear the sound of something cracking. Frozen, you cry out as your feet drop out from under you. The rock beneath you splits and gives way. You tumble down the steep slope and finally land on the edge of a sharp cliff. Your leg is broken. You yell for help, but only your voice echoes in the mountains. No one is coming for you.

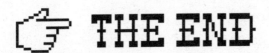 **THE END**

You decide to travel with William's wagon train. You're hopeful you'll be able to convince Tatsa to come along.

You pull Tatsa aside. "It'll be much safer going with them. Please reconsider it? We can get through the Barlow Road on their wagon train. Otherwise, we'd have to sneak around it on foot. We'll save time and food. We could even go off on our own after the tollgate."

She shakes her head firmly. "I don't like this. If you go with them, I will go on alone."

"I'm sorry." Your stomach wrenches. "But I think this is the better option."

"You're wrong."

"Please, Tatsa?"

Finally, she throws her hands up and frowns. "I guess this is where we part ways!"

Your eyes tear up as she walks away. Your stomach

sinks as you slowly climb into Smith's wagon and start off. Snap runs beside the team of six oxen.

"Now . . ." William holds the reigns. "We just passed Three Island Crossing. To be honest, we've gotten a little turned around in this area. Countryside all starts to look the same after a while."

"Well, I have a map!" You reach into your pocket and unfold it. "From what it looks like, we should stay to the north, near the mountains if we can. Our trail guide back on my own wagon train said that if we stray to the south, the road will be dry and difficult."

William nods, but he doesn't take your map, much less glance at it. He seems confident that he'll lead the wagon train in the right direction despite what he just told you.

The road becomes hot and dusty, and William's wagon train rides in circles searching for water.

You should've trusted Tatsa. Your trek ends here.

THE END

You decide to look for food. You're absolutely famished. You've finally got a decent fire going, and it'll be likely another hour before it gets completely dark. The fire will keep while you try to forage for more berries—or grubs, if you have to. You've heard stories about people eating cattails. That doesn't sound appetizing, but neither does eating bugs.

After throwing more twigs onto the fire, you head off into the hills. You're careful to stay within sight of the fire's glow. The last thing you want is to lose your fire. You find waxy red berries—wax currants—and pick as many as you can. Then, raindrops start to fall. You run for cover under a pine tree and wait until it passes.

You've wandered off too far from your fire. Your stomach still howls with hunger.

You see smoke in the distance and you run back to find your kindling charred and smoking. You desperately try to fan the embers, but it's too late. You collect more resin, but that doesn't help.

You don't want to waste the few precious matches you have left, but right now the only thing that matters is staying alive and warm. Hastily, you fumble to strike another match, but your fingers are chilled to the bone and numb. The matchbox slips out of your hand into a puddle.

As you reach to pick it up, the sky opens up into a downpour. It's too dark, and you have no dry kindling or matches left.

You should have built a shelter to keep yourself warm and protected for the night. There is no way you'll get to Oregon City now.

 **THE END**

You decide to reveal yourself. As much as you're afraid of strangers, you dread being alone more.

Before you can move out from behind the tree, the girl turns in your direction. "You can come out. I know you're there."

Your cheeks grow hot. She'd never looked up once. How did she know you were standing there? So much for your tracking skills. You emerge from the trees and stand there awkwardly. "Hello." You fumble with your hands. "I'm sorry, I just wasn't sure if it was safe. I've been traveling alone for some time now."

The girl doesn't respond. She continues to dig along the rocky shore of the river near pieces of driftwood.

"How'd you know I was there?"

"You're pretty loud." She smiles.

"What? Really?"

The girl glances over her shoulder. "Really. You've got a heavy footstep. You think you were watching me? No. I've been following *you* for two days now."

Snap bounds out into the clearing and licks the

girl, his tail wagging wildly. She smiles and puts her hand out for him to smell her scent before she pets him.

This girl seems nice, even if she has been tracking you for the past few days.

"Why were you following me?"

"I'm traveling alone too."

"Before you found me, did you happen to come upon a wagon train?" For a second, you fill with hope.

"There are many traveling on the Trail, but I haven't seen one for about a month." She picks up a piece of driftwood.

You frown, thinking of your family, but then perk up a bit and introduce yourself. You ask for the girl's name.

She pauses for a moment. "Tatsa. It means 'summer' in Shoshone."

You smile. "Pleased to meet you, Tatsa. What are you doing in the middle of the woods, traveling alone?"

"I'm trying to reach Oregon

Territory to find my remaining relatives there. I had been traveling with other family, including my older brother Dommo. Everyone, save for me, died. Overwhelmed with disease from passing fur trappers."

You swallow. "Smallpox."

"I barely survived." Tatsa looks you in the eye. "My mother and father went on ahead to Oregon Territory weeks ago. They've set up their own trading post to trade with the white men and women, and Dommo and I were to join them later on. I've got to find them." She looks down and presses her sharp stick into a small hole in the ground. "I've traveled farther distances before."

"By yourself?"

"No, but it will not be that much different. I've been on my own for several weeks. I have not spoken with another person. The quiet has been nice, but I miss people."

"Is there a chance you'd want to travel together?" You hope she says yes. You could travel part of the way with each other, or at least until you find your wagon train again.

"Why do you think I was following you?" She stops on the shore. "We are two young people traveling alone. It is always better to travel in groups."

You sigh, relieved. "I agree. Do you know the best way to get to Fort Hall from here?"

"I know this area well. I am of the Agaidika Shoshone Nation. My family and I used to live near the Salmon River, in the valley, where food is plentiful. I won't be stopping at Fort Hall, though. Do you still want to travel together?"

What if your family is waiting for you at Fort Hall? On the other hand, the prospect of continuing to travel alone is worse than anything else. You decide quickly. "Yes. I'd be happy to come with you, Tatsa."

She nods, looking just as relieved as you are. "I'm glad to have company. It will be safer with the two of us together. Your dog will also warn against predators."

Then something hits the ground only inches away from you. You kneel and stare down at a ball of ice as large as your fist. More balls of ice start to fall around you.

"Hail!" You leap to your feet. "We need to find cover!" You start for the nearest pine tree.

"No, not that way!" Tatsa runs. "Follow me! I have a better idea!"

You're panicking. What should you do?

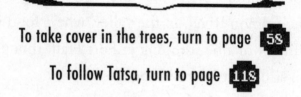

To take cover in the trees, turn to page **58**

To follow Tatsa, turn to page **118**

You decide to jump in and cool off in the pond. After your long trek down Laurel Hill, you're hot and sweaty. Flies and beetles buzz around your head. Now that you are out of the mountains, the air is sticky. The thought of remaining in these filthy clothes is too disgusting. You need a bath, and badly.

You kick off your moccasins and dive into the deeper part of the water, fully submerging your head. The warm water feels good against your skin. You swim around for a few minutes, scrubbing your arms and face, and finally emerge in drenched clothes. You wring out your buckskin tunic and shake out your hair.

Tatsa stands by the edge of the water. Usually she's the first one in—warm or cold, rain or shine.

"You're not coming in?"

She shakes her head slowly. "No, I think not."

Uncertainty flickers through you. "Why not?"

"The water is still. Not good to wash in." She frowns down at the pond, dragging a hand through it. "I would not bathe in this water if I were you."

"It's a bit late for that." A breeze sweeps over the valley, and you shiver in your wet clothes, collapsing by the side of the pond. You feel pain in your leg and pull up your legging. There's a bad scratch running down your calf—probably from the trek across Laurel Hill. It burns badly, and it looks very red and swollen.

Chills run through your body. You huddle into yourself, wishing you'd waited longer before diving into the water.

"Here." Tatsa hands you a blanket. "You look cold."

"I'm fine." You wrap the blanket tightly around yourself. "I just need to warm up."

She doesn't look convinced. "Should we go on? Your clothing will dry sooner if you're moving."

Walking is the last thing you feel like doing with the pain in your leg. "Actually, I'm a little tired," you lie. "Maybe . . . we could stop here for the afternoon to catch our breath and rest? Snap can catch us a rabbit."

"We should really keep moving." Tatsa looks off into the distance. "If you need time to rest, that's fine. Stay and dry off in the sun. I'll go hunting  with Snap." She takes her bow and quiver out of her pack and disappears into the woods with Snap bounding at her heels.

You sit there in the sun, hoping it will warm you up. As the afternoon wears on, your chills only get worse. Soon you're trembling and your forehead is burning up. Your leg throbs. You wish Tatsa would come back soon.

Eventually, she returns with two rabbits. As she gets closer to you, she can see that you're in distress. "Oh no. You don't look well."

"I'm fine," you insist. "Really. I just . . . need more rest."

"I wish you didn't jump into that water. We could have boiled it and washed in it afterward." Tatsa pulls out a pot she found alongside the Trail. You wish she had told you this sooner, but you've both been dehydrated and exhausted.

When she cooks the rabbits, you can only force a few pieces down. Chills rack your body, and pain shoots up your leg to your knee.

"We should move on. It will be dark soon. We need to find a clean water source and better ground to make our camp for the night." Tatsa puts out the fire.

You place a hand over your hidden wound. Should you ignore your increasing pain and feverish state, or tell Tatsa about your injury?

To ignore your illness, turn to page **96**

To tell Tatsa, turn to page **131**

After careful deliberation, you finally tell Tatsa and Bawagap that you would love to accept their invitation to stay in the village.

Tatsa and her family are so excited that you've decided to stay.

"We'll ride horses and also fish and dance and move our village when the seasons change." Tatsa smiles. "You will not regret your decision—I promise."

"No. I don't think I will."

While the idea of never seeing your parents again fills you with sadness, the West is so massive and filled with dangerous and treacherous paths. Life is hard on the Trail, and many people die. Injuries, sickness, animal attacks: to travel the Oregon Trail is to accept the risks involved.

In the end, you know you'll be happy here with Tatsa and her family. Tatsa has already become like a sister to you—the sibling you've never had. The Agaidika Shoshone have welcomed you with open arms, and you haven't felt this at home in a long time.

Your journey on the Oregon Trail ends here.

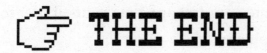 **THE END**

You stumble to your feet and drag yourself over to an enormous pine tree.

"Come on!" Tatsa waves her arm. You see her jumping down into some kind of hole. She motions at you. "Hurry!"

With Snap yelping and Tatsa shouting at you to follow her, you're completely disoriented. The tree doesn't provide the protection you need. Hail pummels down all around you. Thunder booms, and lightning strikes down only feet away. One hailstone hits you on the shoulder, and you fall to the ground with a cry.

You sink back against the tree trunk and huddle into a tight ball. Your arm is on fire; it might even be broken. You wish you'd followed Tatsa.

Suddenly, a hailstone the size of a baseball knocks you in the head. You are concussed, and it will be days before you wake up. Your journey ends here.

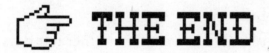 **THE END**

You take Tatsa's advice. The fire glows temptingly, but you listen to Tatsa and keep your distance. You need your feet.

It's torture, but your body warms up slowly. You wonder if you'll ever stop shivering. Your teeth clack.

Tatsa finally returns, but with no food. Snap hangs his head.

"You won't be able to walk for another few days, at least. You were under the snow for hours. I'll head out to hunt again after I warm up a bit." Tatsa pulls off another large piece of tree bark from a nearby pine and lays it over the snow for both of you to sit on.

You start to rub the skin.

"Don't!"

"Why?" You pull back, startled.

"That can make it worse." She kneels and tries to fan hot air onto your skin. Still, you feel nothing.

Tatsa peels off the bandage. When she pulls back, her eyes widen. "Oh no." You both gasp in horror. Your toes have turned a purplish-black, spreading down to the rest of your foot.

"Gangrene." Tatsa's face fills with fear.

Soon, you have no feeling in your foot. There's no cure.

Your hard-fought journey on the Trail ends here.

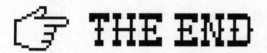 **THE END**

You'll let the fire die out. You're getting colder by the minute. You need to build a shelter, but you also don't want to risk any wayward sparks shooting out and setting your clothes on fire. You huddle near the lowering flames and ignore your hunger. Finally, you fall into an uneasy sleep.

⭐ ⭐ ⭐

In the morning, you wake up ice-cold, but at least you are dry. The fire has fully died out. You check to see how many matches you have left—only four. You'll need to conserve them or find another way to light a fire. Buck Sanders always carried flint and steel, just in case. Now you know why. You wish you had that. Maybe you can find a way to recreate that effect by banging sharp rocks over dry kindling.

Right now you need to find water—and food. Your energy is very low and you feel another headache beginning to form. In searching for your wagon train, you've lost track of the river. You won't last more than a day or two without drinkable water.

You try to retrace your steps. After hours of looking, you finally stumble across a small river— much smaller than Little Wind River. It's shallow, and you could cross it easily. You drink heavily and stop to rest.

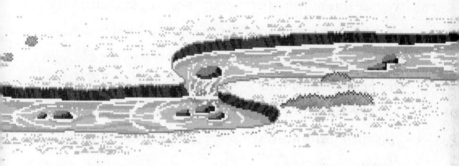

You follow the river for the next few days. You devour anything remotely edible in sight: dandelions, white flowers growing among the rocks—even bugs when you're desperate. You've become so weak and ravenous that you can hardly imagine taking one more step. Then, you realize that you've wandered out of the rocky hills—you've been walking into a flatter prairie for the past several hours.

Uneasiness flutters through your stomach. You stop and look around at the nothingness around you. Today is the first day that the sun has shone for a full day since you became separated from your wagon train. You check your location and stifle the oncoming panic. Now you have absolutely no idea where the Oregon Trail is . . . or how to get back to the nearest landmark.

The sound of a horn catches your attention, and you turn around to see several small wagons in the distance.

"Hey!" You wave wildly. "Hey, I'm here! I'm

here!" You bolt across the prairie toward them. It's your parents—they've found you!

As you run closer, you see that it's not your wagon train. It's an entirely different group of people. You nearly collapse upon reaching the wagon train captain and his family, all of whom are startled by your arrival.

You learn that they are not going west when the wagon train captain, Sam Jones, tells you that they're headed back East to Independence, Missouri. They've encountered too much hardship along the way, and everyone has voted to return home.

"Come with us, if you want." Sam tips his hat. "If you have relatives back East, you can stay with them and write to your folks. They'll get your letter once they reach Oregon City."

You're not sure what to do. You do have aunts and uncles back East, but you still want to find your parents. What should you do?

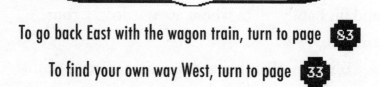

To go back East with the wagon train, turn to page **83**

To find your own way West, turn to page **33**

You tell Tatsa that you should find another water source and she agrees.

"*Fish* don't even drink gray water," she jokes.

As you continue down into the green valley, you find another creek with clear water. You both drink heartily, Tatsa fills up her waterskin, and you rest under the shade of the trees. You catch trout for dinner and roast it over the fire.

"I think we're close now." Tatsa looks at the map. "My parents have a trading station just outside Oregon City. We should reach it within the next few days."

You smile. "I hope so."

Over the next couple of days, you make your way out of the Cascades, heading due west, into rolling foothills. Soon enough, you find yourselves in a lush valley rich with flowers, trees, and meadows. You start to see farmhouses dotting the landscape. You

come across a large farmhouse with a hanging sign that reads TRADING POST. Tatsa stops short, staring hard at a woman tending to the garden in front of the house. Suddenly, she lets out a cry.

"Pia! Pia!" She rushes forward to embrace her mother tightly. They sob, overjoyed. Tears spring to your eyes at the emotional reunion. A tall man comes running from the stables at the noise and stops in his tracks before rushing to hug his daughter. "Appü," Tatsa hugs him.

You wipe your eyes. You're so happy that your dear friend has finally found her parents.

After a long time of hugs and tearful, joyful reunions, Tatsa turns to you and motions you to join them. "Come meet my parents!"

Tatsa pulls you into a hug with her mother and father.

"Pia, Appü, this is my good friend who's helped me get to you." Tatsa takes your hand. "We've traveled on foot for a month or so, after . . . after Dommo and the rest of our family died." Her eyes drop.

Pia looks at Appü, their joy turning to utter dismay. "Our sweet boy." They hold each other, grieving their loss.

After a moment, Tatsa's mother wipes her face and touches your shoulder gently. "Thank you. We're so happy to have our daughter back with us. You must stay and rest and eat. We want to know all that's happened to you."

In the end, you stay with Tatsa's family longer than you expected. You love her and her parents so much, you almost don't want to leave.

★ ★ ★

One morning nearly a week after your arrival, you're helping Tatsa with chores in the house when you see Tatsa's mother talking with a family from a wagon train just outside. She's selling them goods for the final leg of their journey. Maybe they have heard something about your parents. You race outside and catch the family as they're loading up their wagon.

"Excuse me!" You gasp for breath. "I'm sorry to bother you, but did you ever happen to meet a John and Anna Winters on the Oregon Trail?"

"No, I'm afraid not." The woman frowns. "Our own wagon train was decimated by cholera early on. We've barely made it to this point."

Your heart sinks as you watch them leave. Now you wonder if your parents ever made it out of the river near South Pass.

You tell Tatsa your concerns, but she shakes her head. "There are so many pioneers on their way to Oregon City. What are the real chances that they would know your parents?"

You chew on your lip. "I suppose that's true."

"And if there's nothing for you in Oregon City . . ."—Tatsa spreads her arms—"stay here, with us."

Your eyes widen. "Really?"

"Of course," she says matter-of-factly. "You are

family now. My parents know that. If you find you don't want to continue on to Oregon City, then stay and make a life here with us."

You smile, but you're torn. What should you do?

To stay with Tatsa's family, turn to page **103**

To keep going on the Oregon Trail, turn to page **105**

In a state of panic, you can only think of running in the opposite direction of the tumbling snow. The approaching avalanche bears down on you and Tatsa. Tatsa scrambles and swims with the wave of snow, screaming at you to follow her and swim, too. Then, the roar in your ears muffles her voice.

Before you know it, you're swept away by the avalanche. You're knocked unconscious almost immediately.

You wake up freezing cold. Someone shouts in your ears. Everything hurts, and everything feels numb. The next thing you know, a hand is pulling you out of the ice and snow.

"Stay with me!"

Tatsa huddles near you.

Snap's shockingly warm tongue licks at your cheeks. They burn and tingle.

It's only when Tatsa sets you by a large, roaring fire that you realize something terrifying: you can't feel your feet or hands. While the rest of your body begins to revive near the flames, your fingers and toes remain completely numb. Tatsa removes your frozen moccasins and wraps your feet and hands in loose strips of a blanket. She orders you to keep away from the fire. She's placed tree bark underneath you to protect you from the snow.

"I n-need to get them w-warm." Your teeth clatter. "Too c-cold . . ."

"No, I have seen this happen before. If you heat your limbs now and they become cold again afterward, you will lose them to rot and decay. You will not be able to walk again. Is that what you want?"

You shake your head irritably.

"Your hands and feet need to warm up gradually, and *stay* warm. So keep them away from the fire. Close, but not too close." Tatsa grabs her bow and rises to her feet. "I need

to find us food. It'll help us warm up on the inside."
She disappears into the forest.

You sit near the fire and close your eyes as the icy
cold air blows in your face. No matter how hard you
try, you can't seem to get warm. Huddling onto your
knees, you stare glumly over at the crackling fire.

It couldn't be a bad thing to just put your feet
close to the fire for a *little* while, at least, could it?
For just a few minutes, just until they're not numb
anymore.

You look around. Tatsa is no longer in sight. She's
had far more experience out in the cold wilderness
than you. Your thinking is clouded by your dropping
body temperature. The parts of you that aren't numb
just ache.

Should you get closer to the fire for a little while,
or listen to Tatsa's advice?

To put your feet close to the fire, turn to page **23**

To listen to Tatsa's advice, turn to page **60**

Finding shelter is the most important thing right now. Although your survival skills are basic, you remind yourself that you just traveled a thousand miles on foot. This gives you a boost of confidence. Your body can wait at least a few more hours to find food. It's almost dark out, so building a lean-to is critical to surviving the night. It'll keep you and your fire protected from the rain.

You pick a good spot surrounded by tall pines to build a temporary shelter. You pick the sturdiest tree nearest the fire and start searching for long,  thick branches to prop up against the trunk. About half an hour later, you have enough branches.

You place them one by one against the windward side of the tree so that your shelter and fire won't get destroyed by the mountain gusts. You weave the smaller branches together to lock them in place. You plaster piles of dirt you've dug up from the forest floor and wet leaves onto the walls to keep heat in. Inside, you pile up a small mattress of leaves, moss, and twigs to protect yourself from the cold ground.

Thunder rumbles overhead, and rain starts falling not long after you complete your lean-to. You huddle inside and cover yourself with leaves. Your stomach growls louder and louder, but you know you made the right decision. You'll survive the night and forage for food in the morning.

Exhausted and bone-weary, you place a log on your fire, curl up in your shelter, and fall into a deep sleep.

When you wake up the next morning, the storm clouds and rain have given way to a fresh, clear sunrise. All that's left of your fire is black carbon and ash.

With your hunger more immediate than ever, you grab a walking stick from your lean-to and go off in

search of more berries and flowers to eat. You come
upon some bushes filled with red waxy berries—wax
currants. They're bitter and tangy on your tongue, but
you eat as many as you can. As you continue to clean
the bushes of their berries, you see a small lake nearby.
Birds and several squirrels are drinking from it.

You're parched, but you shouldn't drink water
that has been sitting stagnant and still.

You hear water flowing as you walk closer to the
lake.

A river!

It might be the Little Wind River, but you are
too disoriented to know for sure. It's much tamer
now that the storm has passed. You walk down to
the bank, drink your fill, and wash your face. You've

found a section that is very narrow, with stones protruding from the water. If only your wagon train had come this way. You hush the thought and carefully step on the stones to cross the river.

There's no time to waste. You need to keep moving, even if being lost in these mountains feels hopeless. You have no idea where your wagon train is at this point. You've got to get back on the Oregon Trail.

You head northwest. With the sun leaning to one side of the morning sky, you know to move in the opposite direction. You hope you'll catch up with your wagon train in the mountains. Traveling alone, you don't need to worry about hauling heavy wagons

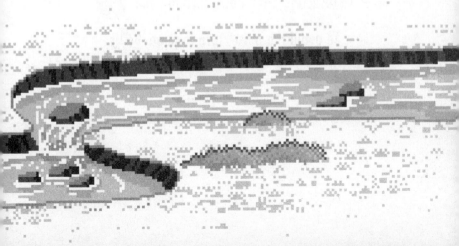

and teams of tired oxen. You're moving at a quicker pace.

With a newfound determination, you take one last drink from the river and gather two good handfuls of wax currants. You roll them up in aspen leaves and put them in your pockets. You start off on your journey again.

You've walked for several hours, stopping whenever you see berries or currants. Out of the blue you hear a bone-chilling howl nearby. It sounds like your dog, Snap. Should you investigate further or avoid it?

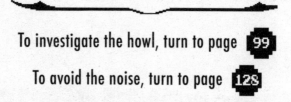

To investigate the howl, turn to page **99**

To avoid the noise, turn to page **128**

While you want nothing more than to reach Oregon City to reunite with your parents, you're still very weak and sick. You can hardly sit upright, much less travel in a bumpy wagon.

You turn to Tatsa. "I think . . . I think I shouldn't go anywhere. I need to stay here. At least for a little while." Your speech is slurred.

Tatsa nods solemnly. "I agree. You wouldn't make it another mile the way you are."

When you tell Smith's wagon train that you won't be going with them, they're confused, but not terribly disappointed. You can tell they don't want to be traveling with someone who's injured. You can't blame them. You watch their little wagon train disappear into the trees.

"You shouldn't feel like you have to stay behind for me, Tatsa." You frown and look at the ground. "I know you want to see your family again. And we're . . . so close. You should go on. If you want to."

Tatsa reaches for your hand. "I won't leave you. I will stay until you recover."

You're grateful for her companionship.

While you'd hoped that resting in the Tenino village would help you fully recover, you become progressively weaker. Your dreams of reuniting with your family in Oregon City are squashed.

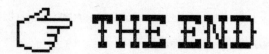 **THE END**

The best option is to travel back East with this wagon train to Independence, Missouri. From there, you'll continue back home to St. Louis to find your uncle Benjamin and aunt Sally. They were heartbroken when you and your parents decided to move West. You are very lucky to have them. They'll take you in when you get back.

Still, you feel lost without your parents. In a last-ditch effort, you ask Sam if he's seen any other wagon trains passing through this area within the past week.

He shakes his head. "Can't say I have, I'm afraid. We've gotten pretty turned around ourselves more than once. If your parents were looking for you, they might've gotten lost in the mountains nearby north, or maybe just kept going."

That settles it. You return East with the wagon train to reunite with your other relatives. You can only hope you'll see your parents again someday.

☞ **THE END**

You decide to stand your ground, even though you want to turn tail and flee into the woods. But it's better to stay facing a predator head-on and challenge them if you can. You strike your walking stick firmly into the ground and glare at the wolf closest to you.

The three wolves still draw closer. But then, the leader pauses. He snaps his fangs and snarls.

You don't move.

An agonizingly long moment passes. One strike and you're dead meat. In the distance, you hear the cry of the elk. It looks like those wolves got their meat. Maybe now they won't want you.

Finally the wolves turn away and retreat into the woods.

You let out a slow sigh, feeling the beat of your heart pounding against your chest. You thought you were a goner.

Just as you think the coast is clear . . .

A blur of copper-and-white fur bolts into the clearing. You can hardly believe your eyes. It can't be.

"Snap!" you cry. Your beloved pup stumbles in between you and the wolves, barking wildly. You're horrified to see that one of his legs is bleeding.

Just as the wolves are slinking off into the woods, one turns its head at the sound of Snap's yelping.

"Snap, quiet!" you hiss frantically. "Shush!"

The wolves trot back and close in on you and your dog. You know it's over.

☞ **THE END**

You help the woman and her family.

"I can't carry more than one person with me, ma'am." You gesture toward your horse. "Not safely, anyway. I can take one child, but it would be better for you if I hurried to get a doctor in Oregon City. It's not far."

She fervently shakes her head. "No, no! By the time the doctor comes back, my husband will be dead—and so will my children! You must take us with you!"

"I *can't*—"

"Then take my youngest!" She heaves up her youngest child toward your saddle. "At least one of us should make it!"

You awkwardly grasp the coughing little boy in your arms. He starts to cry and tries to wiggle back for his mother.

"Just go! Hurry!" She slaps your horse's flanks and you gallop off toward Oregon City. You hold the little boy tightly with one arm and the reins in the other.

You feel uneasy balancing on the horse. Then, you notice a rash on the little boy's face.

When you reach the city later that day, you're exhausted and feverish. You find the doctor and he immediately puts you both to bed. He assures you that another doctor will ride out to help the boy's family.

You sleep for a long time. Your fever and cough only get worse. A few days after that, you're covered in the same red spots as the little boy. You made it to Oregon City, but you never find your family. A case of measles gets the best of you.

 **THE END**

As much as I'd like to stay here, we need to keep moving on. I've got to cross the mountains along the Barlow Road soon. I'm still hopeful that I'll catch up with my family there."

Tatsa nods. "It's been a welcome respite, but I am anxious to rejoin my parents too."

You and Tatsa pack up the supplies provided by her family: blankets for the cold weather up ahead, a map found on the Trail, and lots of food, like dried meat, chokeberry pies, dried salmon, and plenty of camas roots to boil. Aunt Bawagap has even gifted you with a brand-new beaded buckskin tunic, leggings trimmed with rabbit fur, and soft moccasins for the remainder of your journey. _"Aise! Aise!"_ You thank her profusely in Shoshone—Tatsa taught you—grateful that you've made such kind new friends.

While the village can't spare any horses, you've grown so used to walking and don't mind much. You and

Tatsa say goodbye to the Shoshone village and start
alongside the Salmon River. It is a barren landscape
with nothing in sight but sandy brown hills and cliffs
covered in scrub brush. It's damp and chilly, even
in the middle of summer, and the wind whips your
clothes. You both wrap your new blankets tightly
around you.

You and Tatsa stop to fish for fresh salmon and
trout from the river to roast over the fire.

As you walk, the tree-capped hills grow barren
and dusty. The country flattens into a wavy, desert-
like brown landscape. You look at the map and
wonder if you've passed Fort Boise already. You think
you might be near Three Island Crossing, but you're
not sure. Then, you finally see it: a winding river in
the near distance.

"Snake River!" Tatsa rushes off toward the water,
Snap bounding at her heels. "Come on, slowpoke!"

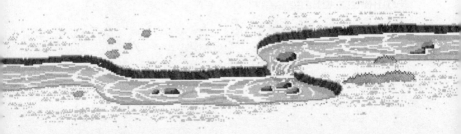

You start after her, but as you turn to survey the landscape, something catches your eye. You squint in the sun and gasp. You can hardly believe your eyes. It's a wagon train!

Your heart leaps. Is it *your* wagon train? You start running to meet them, not realizing Tatsa has stopped behind you.

As you draw closer, your heart sinks. You scan the following wagons—none of the people are your parents. You swallow your disappointment and wave back as the wagon train captain calls a halt.

"Hello there!" the wagon train captain calls. He dismounts the wagon and his feet hit the ground. "I'm William Smith. What are you doing out here alone?" He eyes your clothing curiously.

"We're trying to reach Oregon City to find our

families. I was separated from my wagon train back
near South Pass, and Tatsa lost most of her family due
to sickness."

"You've made it all this way alone?" William's
eyebrow arches.

"The two of us, yes."

He puts his hand on his hip. "You can't be older
than . . ."

"Twelve, sir," you say. "Thirteen later this year.
But . . . you wouldn't happen to have met a John and
Anna Winters on the Trail, would you?"

He shakes his head slowly. "Can't say that I did."

"What about a loud guy named Buck Sanders?
Their wagon train captain?"

William frowns. "Sorry."

You bite your lip, disappointed.

"Well, hey," says William. "It's not safe for you
two to be out here on your own. Any number of foul
folk are taking advantage of pioneers on the Trail.
What say you come with us?"

You turn to Tatsa. "That might be nice?"

Tatsa takes you aside. "Listen. The Shoshone have

always been friends to any travelers that pass through our lands, but I can't risk getting sick. I lost Dommo and almost my entire family—I barely made it. You can go, but you will have to go on without me. I just don't have a good feeling about this."

Traveling with a wagon train might be safer. You wouldn't have to worry about hunting food as much as you do. Maybe you'd catch up to your wagon train? But you trust Tatsa and her instincts. Should you ride along with the wagon train or keep traveling with Tatsa?

To go with the wagon train, turn to page **42**

To keep traveling with Tatsa, turn to page **36**

You join Smith's wagon train this time. Despite your weeks-long fatigue and recovering injury, you're desperate for your chance to make it to Oregon City, and you decide to take it.

"I have to try, Tatsa." You look her in the eye. "I wish you would come with me."

She's already shaking her head. "No. I'd rather not. I am doing just fine without a wagon train."

"You're okay going on alone?"

"Yes. Also, several Tenino people have said they are going to try to make their way in Oregon City themselves. I will travel with them until I find my family."

You wish you could go with them, but you want to travel by wagon. Your legs are exhausted, and your wound still throbs. "I'm sorry we have to part like this. But I hope you find your family."

She leans forward to hug you. "When you reunite with your family, come and find us. You will always be welcome in our home."

You swallow back tears. You depart with Smith's wagon train the next morning, a new uneasiness settling over you. Most of the wagon train members resent your presence. They avoid you, as none of them want to catch the infection. In addition, the wagon's bumpiness only makes your leg pain worse. You have to stop often to adjust your bandages.

Despite many days of rest, your tired body gives out to exhaustion in the end. Your trek on the Trail ends here.

 **THE END**

You ignore what your body is telling you. Your leg throbs with every step, but you know Tatsa is right about moving on. You're getting so close to Oregon City. Maybe if you walk it off, it'll be fine. When Tatsa casts you an odd look, you shake your head and wave her off.

"I'm fine. We are so close. Let's keep going."

She studies you. "Are you sure? You don't look like yourself."

You smile weakly. "I'm fine, Tatsa. Really. I just need to keep moving."

"You hardly ate anything. You said you were hungry. We should rest here longer," Tatsa says.

"No. No, let's move on." You feel dizzy. Tatsa jumps up and grabs your arm. Snap yelps.

You wrap a blanket around your shivering body. You haven't felt this weak in a long time.

You continue into a lush green valley

surrounded by rocky hills on either side. Your feet sink into the ground with each step.

Finally, you can't continue on. Agony overtakes you, and you double over into the grass. Tatsa shouts in alarm as you collapse to the ground.

"Why did you not say something earlier?" She touches your clammy forehead. "You are gravely ill!"

You admit that you didn't want to feel like a burden. When you tell her about your leg wound, she cleans it and wraps it in a bandage.

She places her hands on her hips. "This wound does not look good."

You soon fall into a feverish state. Sadly, your journey West ends here.

 **THE END**

You decide to cook the animal. At this point, you've been foraging for food well into the afternoon. You and Snap are both starving. Eating something that's been dead and rotting for a while is dangerous, but your appetite takes over. You use one of your last matches to strike up a fire and roast the animal over a spit. It didn't smell good before, but the odor of rotted, burnt carcass is even less appetizing.

Still. It's food, and you need to eat. You and Snap devour what's left of the deer.

As you drift off to sleep, nausea rises up in your gut. Within hours, you're so ill that you can't even lift your head. Your search for your family and Oregon City ends here.

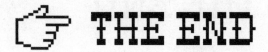 **THE END**

You investigate the howl. The whimpering echoes through the trees, sending a shiver down your spine. It could be an injured wolf . . . or it could be Snap. The two of you got separated days ago. Maybe he was swept down the river too. Maybe he's hurt.

You go and look—carefully. You take your small knife out of your pocket just in case. Gently pushing through the brush, you back up against a large pine tree. Whimpers and sounds of scuffling nearby make you hesitate. You start to second-guess your decision.

You hold your knife tightly and peer around the tree. You gasp when you see the creature struggling in a thorny thicket.

"Snap!"

Your beloved dog looks up at the sound of your voice and barks happily. You rush forward, ignoring the thorns scratching at your  clothing and arms, and kneel to hug Snap. He whimpers and covers your face with licks.

"I've never been so happy to see you." Tears prick your eyes. "I'm so glad I found you."

You're not alone anymore! You don't recall ever feeling such elation or relief in your life.

"Don't worry." You try to calm him down. "I'll get you out of this." You gently unwind the vines from around his ear and carefully pull out several thorns. He whimpers but doesn't move. "We need to find you water. C'mon, boy. Let's go."

Even though Snap's heavy, you pick him up and set him down once you're safely out of the thicket. You find a tiny brook running through the rocky forest terrain. You wash his torn ear, tear off a strip of your sleeve, and bandage it.

After eating the last of your wax currants and sipping water from the brook, you're still so hungry. Snap licks his own chops.

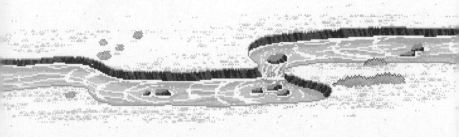

Time to hunt!

You've hunted rabbits and prairie
dogs with Snap before. He's got a keen
sense of smell when chasing down
quick jackrabbits.

You follow Snap as he trots through the rocky
terrain, his nose to the ground. Then, he lifts his
head, his nose and floppy ears twitching. A flash of
gray darts across the forest floor. He bolts!

You want to race after him, but your legs are
tired. You trust Snap. He's a determined hunter, and
in the end, the rabbit is just too slow for him.

You build a fire using tree resin and
one of your matches after gathering
kindling and small sticks. You hang
the rabbit hide out to dry to use
as a waterskin—your canteen is
lost in the river somewhere.

After a short rest, it's time to travel on. You
extinguish the flames—the last thing you want to do
is start a forest fire. You continue on your journey. As

the afternoon wears on, you realize that you've passed the same oddly shaped tree twice now. You've been walking in circles. Should you hike to higher ground to see where you are, or start following the nearby brook downstream to lower ground?

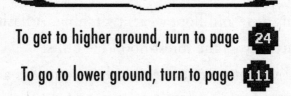

To get to higher ground, turn to page **24**

To go to lower ground, turn to page **111**

You choose to stay with Tatsa's family, even though you're so close to Oregon City and possibly reuniting with your parents. You've heard nothing of your parents' wagon train since the day you got lost. Talking to various wagon trains has discouraged you and only solidified your decision. You're not sure where your parents are, or if they're still alive. But the idea of getting to Oregon City and winding up alone, with no support or friends, doesn't seem like an appealing life to live. You know this is the best decision.

In the back of your mind, you're still hoping that your parents will find you someday.

You'll make it to Oregon City at some point, but for now, you're content to live at the trading post with Tatsa and her parents. Your journey to Oregon City stops here.

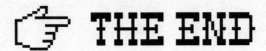 **THE END**

You keep going on the Trail.

Tatsa nods solemnly at your decision.

You hug her. "I'll be back to visit, I promise. And if I don't find my parents, I'll come back—for good."

"I'd like that. Our home is always open to you. And I think you will find your parents. I have a feeling in here." She presses a hand to her chest.

You hope she's right.

The next morning, you say a heartfelt goodbye to Tatsa and her family.

According to your map, Oregon City isn't far at all. It's an even quicker journey thanks to the horse that Tatsa's family has given you—or lent you, Tatsa has joked, because you'll be back to visit. With a fresh bedroll, food, and a bit of money from Tatsa's parents, you start off on your final leg of the Oregon Trail, both nervous and anticipating a possible reunion.

As the day wears on, you realize

how much you miss Tatsa. Snap trudges alongside you, his head hung low. You know he's missing her almost as much as you are.

"I know, boy. I know."

The hilly countryside has given way to flat, lush plains dotted with trees and thick bushes. As you emerge from a grove of trees, your horse suddenly hesitates and pulls on the bridle. You look up to see a lone wagon sitting in the field just up ahead. A woman sits on the ground, rocking children in her arms. When she sees you, she jumps to her feet.

"Help!" The woman waves frantically. "Please, help us!"

You pull on the reins to stop the horse, but your mount doesn't like it. She whickers nervously and steps backwards, her ears twitching.

"Please." There are dark circles under the woman's eyes. She's holding two little children with hollow, empty eyes. "Please help us. My husband is terribly

ill. The rest of our wagon train has died from a
horrible plague. Please take us with you!"

"I . . . I'm not sure I can, ma'am." You don't move
any closer. "I can go get help for you. It's not far to
Oregon City on horseback."

She shakes her head impatiently. "No, no! By
then it'll be too late! You must take us with you, now!
Before we all catch the plague!"

You're not sure what to do. You're fearful of this
contagious disease. Plus, you don't have enough
room on your horse for more than one child, much
less four people. Also . . . you've heard stories about
people posing as injured travelers who take advantage
of unsuspecting people on their way to Oregon City,
robbing them blind. Should you stay to help them, or
get help in Oregon City?

To stay and help, turn to page 87

To get help in Oregon City, turn to page 143

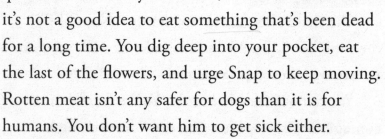

You move on. The sight and foul stench of the deer carcass turns your hunger into queasiness. Even if you cook it, it's not a good idea to eat something that's been dead for a long time. You dig deep into your pocket, eat the last of the flowers, and urge Snap to keep moving. Rotten meat isn't any safer for dogs than it is for humans. You don't want him to get sick either.

Snap whines and whimpers, wagging his tail. You let him go on some yards ahead as he tries to pick out scents to track down.

You follow him out of a thick grove of trees and onto a small grassy, pebbled shore, dipping down into a crystal blue-green lake. After nibbling a bit of grass, Snap rushes into the water and reemerges, shaking himself out. You laugh and hurry to dip your waterskin in the clear water.

You wash your face and drink. Then a great brown mass fills your vision. You look up to see a hulking creature standing in the water only feet away, near thick reeds. The creature swings its head up and stares at you with enormous black eyes, chewing slowly.

It's a moose. Behind her, a gangling calf peers out curiously.

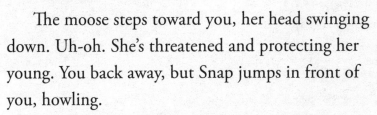

You freeze. Beside you, Snap wags his tail and barks.

"Shush!"

The moose steps toward you, her head swinging down. Uh-oh. She's threatened and protecting her young. You back away, but Snap jumps in front of you, howling.

As you turn to run, you hear a low terrible braying sound. It's deep and intimidating. You can't escape the moose.

 **THE END**

You are disoriented in these mountains—everything is starting to look the same. You move to lower ground. Following the river is the best choice. You hope it'll lead to a bigger water source—and maybe to a wagon train corral.

You walk by short waterfalls and past rocky boulders with patches of moss and wildflowers. You take some to eat later. You also come across thick patches of sagebrush—wonderful, rich-smelling plants that are safe to eat. You fill your pockets.

The sage has such a pleasant aroma.

You pause to make sure that you're not backtracking, and sure enough, you see the sun's location in the sky and are certain you are headed west. You hope that eventually this river will lead you out of the woods and to the mouth of Snake River, an Oregon Trail landmark. From there, you can get to Fort Hall. You still have hopes that your family is waiting for you there. That encouraging thought puts an extra spring in your step as you descend the mountain slope.

Snap catches a small rabbit, which you roast over a fire. After this, you only have one match left. You've been notching holes in pine trees for their resin to fuel the fires, but you're not sure what to do without the spark of a match. You'll have to teach yourself how to use flint and steel. You wish you'd paid closer attention to Mama when she got the campfire going. You know next to nothing about surviving in the wild.

⭐ ⭐ ⭐

The next day when you wake up, Snap is missing. You frantically call for him, but after about half an hour he hasn't returned. You keep walking, shouting and shouting. Finally he comes back through the bushes.

You nearly sob with relief. "Don't do that again!" You pat his head. He licks your hand.

As you keep following the river, Snap lets out a sudden yelp. You peer around a pine tree: a spot of tan with splashes of color amid the shadows of the forest.

It's a girl.

She looks about your age. Her two long braids hang down her shoulders over a beaded buckskin dress. It looks so comfortable and light compared to your thick, dirty clothes. A large pack sits at her feet, and a small fire crackles nearby.

She's facing away from you, digging at the

ground. You watch as she continues to poke around pieces of driftwood near the bank of the river with a pointed stick. She reaches down and pulls out something—a tree root. She pauses and glances back in your direction; you duck behind the tree.

You're about step out from hiding to say hello, but you catch yourself. Maybe that's not the right thing to do. Your short time alone in the mountains has made you especially cautious. Snap noses you with a whimper. You hush him and gently push him back. You need to be cautious.

You haven't spoken to another human being in days. What if she can help you? What if she's friendly? This could be your only chance at surviving. But what if she doesn't want to be bothered? Should you reveal yourself or stay in hiding?

To reveal yourself, turn to page **46**

To stay in hiding, turn to page **40**

You need to search for your wagon train before it gets too dark. Maybe they aren't that far away. You could locate some wheel ruts, follow them, and, with luck, get back on the Trail. From there you'll find South Pass and continue on. Maybe you could join up with another wagon train, at least until you reunite with your family.

The wind picks up. You shiver as the trees rustle around you. Your head still aches. You start your journey down through the hills. It's your best guess about where the wagon train could be headed. It's pitch black outside. Downhill is better than uphill with the weather system moving through. Even if you're backtracking, it's better than getting lost in the mountains.

As you walk, your stomach rumbles with hunger, and your tongue sticks to the roof of your mouth. You're dehydrated. You lost your waterskin during the storm—it held all of your pure water—and there's no spring or brook nearby. You wish you had Snap with you to help hunt for food.

You get dizzier with each step. You trip over a rock and tumble forward, scraping your hands against a boulder. When you finally stand up, you feel sick. Nothing is familiar in the growing darkness. You're lost, you have no food, no water, and now you're injured too.

You need to make a fire before it's too late. You scramble to gather some twigs and finally manage to spark a flame with damp matches and kindling. By the time you have a roaring fire going, you can hardly keep your eyes open, but at least you're warm. Should you add more wood to the fire before you sleep, or let it die out now?

To add more wood to the fire, turn to page **27**

To let the fire die out, turn to page **62**

You decide to follow Tatsa.

"Follow me!" She holds her pack over her head. "It's not safe by the trees! We've got to find shelter!"

You dodge another hailstone and follow her. Snap barks at your side. She ducks into a hole in the ground. You wiggle into the burrow beside her, and pull Snap in too.

"Badger's nest. I found it searching for roots. Trees become top-heavy with the weight of the ice. Look." Tatsa points to a pine tree branch about to crack.

"Good thinking." You wipe your brow.

The hail stops in an instant. You both emerge with some hesitation. Tatsa drops her pack, takes up her sharp stick, and starts poking around near the shores of the river again.

"What are you doing?"

"Digging for camas roots for stew." Tatsa

examines the ground. "Their flowers are bright blue, and the roots are white, no larger than your fingers. They're best found in mouse holes near driftwood. Take a sharp stick and poke around until you find one."

You both dig around for roots. When you finally find some in a small rodent hole, you pluck them out proudly.

"They taste better when you cover them and cook them over a fire pit." Tatsa puts a root in her pocket. "But roasting takes too long. We will just boil them instead."

When Snap catches a squirrel, you all eat well that night. Tatsa teaches you how to start a fire with two sharp flint stones that shower sparks over dry kindling. She knows about the resin trick too. You take turns sleeping to keep watch, feeding the fire through the night.

The next morning, you make your way down into the valley.

"If you don't mind me asking, how'd you learn to speak English, Tatsa?"

"White men have been crossing our land for a long time now. We've had no choice but to learn. It's certain more people will come this way seeking our land."

You kick a nearby pebble. "I never thought about it like that."

She leans over and points to your pocket. "What are those?"

You pull out the flowers. "Oh, these. Rock cress and some other kind of flower. They're good to eat."

She takes a bunch from you and eats it. "I like them. I suppose you're a useful companion after all." She smiles.

⭐ ⭐ ⭐

Over the next few days you climb out of the valley onto gentle hills and prairies. You continue to go northwest for what feels like a week. You think of your family as you stare at a sparkling winding river in the distance.

"See over there. We are close to the Bitterroot Mountains." Tatsa points. "We are close to my Agaidika Shoshone village. The name of our Nation translates roughly to "salmon eaters," given our location in the Salmon River valley."

You're excited to go to Tatsa's village and eat some homecooked food, but you're already dreading climbing those mountains.

Tatsa sees your face and smiles. "Don't worry. There are footpaths that will make the ascent easier."

After hours of trekking on well-worn trails, you finally descend to lower ground and then into the Salmon River valley where you arrive at Tatsa's Agaidika Shoshone village. You stop to take in the breathtaking view of the surrounding Bitterroot Mountains.

Snap darts ahead. Three Shoshone women look up from their work digging for roots near the river's shore. With a second wind, Tatsa rushes to greet them. One woman throws her arms around Tatsa. Tatsa speaks to them quietly, gesturing with her hands, then motions to you. One of the women approaches you and rubs her cheeks against yours. You smile.

"It signifies friendship," Tatsa says, eagerly

introducing you to her aunt Bawagap and her cousins Sanap and Aken.

After a full day of digging for nourishment, you feel accomplished and so honored to meet Tatsa's extended family. At night, surrounded by tall tipis made of willow branches and buffalo hides, everyone shares stories around the fire and eats a hearty meal of roasted salmon, elk, and chokecherry cakes. Tatsa tells you that Lewis and Clark crossed over this valley about forty years ago with Sacagawea, a brave woman from this same Shoshone Nation. Her aunt Bawagap knew her, too. The stories continue and Tatsa translates Shoshone into English so you understand. People laugh and dance. You haven't been this happy in months!

The next day you help Tatsa, Sanap, and Aken with their daily chores, such as drying out elk hides, digging for camas roots, and playing with the children. It's good to be surrounded by a community of people again.

By the fourth day, you wonder if you should keep

moving on. You want to stay longer, but you also still have hope that you'll catch up with your family's wagon train. You desperately miss Mama and Pa. Should you stay a while longer or keep traveling?

To stay longer, turn to page **56**

To keep traveling, turn to page **89**

Eating unfamiliar plant life is not worth the risk of getting sick. After all, you've got Snap with you now. If he can catch another rabbit or squirrel, you'll be set for the next day. You continue pushing through the rocky terrain. You take a long drink from your water skin. You'll have to find water soon, too.

The day drags on with little success. Snap tries and fails to hunt several squirrels, and even pounces on nearby birds. Aside from a measly half-eaten bush of black raspberries and several dandelions, you don't find any real sustenance.

Then Snap suddenly drops his head to the ground. He snorts and trots ahead of you. He lifts his head and stares off into the forest.

"What is it, boy?" You look too.

And then you see it. A pair of tall, twitching brown ears. Black eyes.

A rabbit!

Snap leaps into the bushes after the rabbit. The two of them race until they finally disappear through the trees. You wait to see if the rabbit will come back around, but minutes drag by. Snap's echoing bays turns into whimpers.

"Snap? Snap?" You hurry after him. He finally reemerges from behind a pine tree, his tail drooping.

No rabbit.

You sigh heavily. "Oh, Snap. This one was just too quick for you, was it?" You scratch behind his ears. "I guess we'll have to keep looking, won't we?"

You glance up at the early afternoon sky. It looks like it may rain again. You hold back a groan. This is just your luck.

Then you see it: tufts of grass sticking out from a tree branch, and three golden-brown ovals. Eggs. Eggs would be a delicious meal. It'd be a tricky climb up that pine tree to reach them, but it would be worth it.

"Stay here, Snap." Gripping the bottom branch, you swing yourself up and lean against the trunk. You lift yourself up again, twisting around the tree to step on branches that can support you. As you climb higher, the branches become thinner and more brittle. One snaps underneath your foot. Your heart leaps.

But now the eggs are really close. You edge onto a limb and reach out with one hand.

The branch beneath you gives way. Your dreams of getting to Oregon City give way here too.

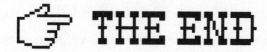 **THE END**

You avoid whatever is making that awful howling noise. The last thing you want is to find yourself face to face with an angry coyote or wolf. Wolves run in packs, and you know you'd never make it against one wolf, much less a whole hungry pack.

You keep moving on. The howls finally fade into the distance. It is odd how much it sounded like your dog, Snap, but you're sure it couldn't have been him.

A twig cracks nearby; you freeze as something moves. A hulking shadow draws closer and you're relieved to find that it's an enormous elk. Elk meat would be delicious and last you a while. Your last few meals have only been berries.

You have your small knife, but it's hardly something that would take down an enormous elk. You'll need to fashion yourself some traps, if not a bow and arrow. You could also make a slingshot out of the flexible bark of a young tree, your string, and a stone.

You look over and the elk is staring at you. It snorts and tosses its antlers. You hope it won't charge at you. You maintain eye contact and take a slow step back.

A snarl from the bushes is your only warning before several gray-and-black furry beings fly out of the trees and descend upon the elk. You're frozen in fear: a pack of wolves!

The elk lets out a shrill shriek and takes off into the forest. Several wolves bound off after it, howling and yapping all the way. Just when you think you're safe, you hear a low growl behind you. You slowly turn to see three toothy wolves only feet away, ready to pounce.

Should you stand your ground and face the wolves down, or run?

To stand your ground, turn to page **85**

To run, turn to page **29**

You tell Tatsa you're injured.

"I don't think I should keep walking, Tatsa." You lift up your legging to reveal your swollen, angry red scratch.

She drops her pack and hurries up to you. "This does not look good."

"What do we do?"

"Clean it out as best we can." She pours water onto your wound. You cry out from the pain and double over. She wraps your calf in a bandage.

"You don't look well at all." Tatsa looks at you.

"I'll be fine." After a moment, you stand up again. You cringe and try to ignore the pain. Exhaustion and dizziness hang over you.

"We will stop here to camp, then," Tatsa says. "Until you're well again."

You only hope that you *will* be well again.

As Tatsa starts a campfire and finds sticks to build a lean-to for the night, you hear a man's voice. You both look up to see several Native American men approaching. Tatsa speaks to them in Shoshone, but they shake their heads, not understanding. She tries words in another indigenous dialect, one you don't recognize.

After some difficult communication, Tatsa relaxes her stance and nods to you.

"These are men of the Tenino People." She introduces you to Yáka, Tl'álk and Nawinalá. "They know you are ill and want to help. Their village is nearby, equipped with food and medicine. I think we should go with them."

You nod weakly. Help would be more than welcome, considering the way you're feeling. Your leg is burning up.

Yáka carries you to their nearby village, next to a

stream. Tatsa murmurs to you that they are a fishing tribe who travel up and down the Columbia River and split their time between winter and summer dwellings.

The kind people lay you down in one of their huts and cover you with a thin blanket. An elderly woman wipes your sweaty neck and forehead and covers your wound with clean bandages every few hours. Pain still lingers, but it has dulled.

A week passes. You think sometimes that you'll never feel well again, but in the second week at camp, you start to improve. One afternoon, you see a familiar wagon train rolling by—it's Smith's. They stop to trade with Yáka, Tl'álk, and Nawinalá, and when the wagon train sees you, they're astonished. They offer again to bring you and Tatsa with them to Oregon City. But you know Tatsa won't want to go

with them. You also know you may need more rest and should stay with Tatsa.

Should you join Smith's wagon train, or stay and rest with Tatsa?

To join Smith's wagon train, turn to page 94

To rest, turn to page 81

You and Tatsa dash to climb the nearest tree. It's a split-second decision. You know that you can't outrun an avalanche. You pick up Snap with one arm and toss him onto the branch above you. Just as you swing up beside Tatsa, the snow slides inches beneath your feet. The tree shudders and shakes. You hold on for dear life—and hope the trunk can withstand the enormous amount of force. Within minutes, the snow stops moving.

You both reluctantly jump down into the snow. Snap buries his nose in the fresh powder and shakes himself off.

You let out a sigh. "That was close."

"Too close." Tatsa pats the bark, and to your surprise, peels off a piece. Then another piece.

"What are you doing?"

She rips off a thick strand of bark and stuffs it in her mouth. "I'm hungry." Tatsa holds a strip out to you. "Try it."

The idea of eating tough, scratchy tree bark isn't appealing, but you take the strip from her. It's not bad. Not great, but still edible—and chewy like jerky. You wish you'd known this earlier.

After hours of traveling down the mountain, the temperature gradually rises and you see deep wagon wheel ruts cover the ground where the snow is melting. Looking ahead, you see a swarm of travelers. You check your map: Barlow Tollgate. You scan the crowd for your parents. No luck. You and Tatsa take advantage of the hustle and bustle, careful to stay out of the distracted tollgate operator's sight.

After about an hour of traveling, you set up camp in a nook surrounded by trees, hunt for and gather food, and then rest for the night as dark falls.

In the morning, you continue on to Laurel Hill. You and Tatsa avoid the main Trail and keep to the thick cover of trees. Traveling in plain sight feels more dangerous.

Finally you reach the bottom of the steep incline

and find yourselves in a warmer, pleasant valley surrounded by thick, lush trees. Just ahead, you spot glistening water: a small pond. You are both hot and sweaty after the climb down Laurel Hill. You and Tatsa hurry toward it, eager to wash your faces. You even want to go swimming.

The water is muddy and stagnant. It smells strange, too. Should you jump into this pond, or find another water source?

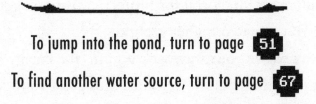

To jump into the pond, turn to page **51**

To find another water source, turn to page **67**

Building a fire is the most important thing to do right now. It's getting dark very quickly and there's no immediate way to track your wagon train down.

The temperature is dropping and you need to light a fire to keep yourself warm. It will also ward off any predators. You shiver at the thought of what lurks in these hills—burly bears, slinking wildcats, white-fanged wolves, poisonous snakes, and gigantic moose.

The storm is passing. Staying in the camp clearing without a wagon corral for protection is not a good idea. You move to higher ground.

You weave your way back up into the craggy hills until you find yourself in a small gulley surrounded by tall trees and rocks. You settle into a nook in between several thick pines. You brush aside wet

leaves and damp twigs to get to the dirt beneath and place several stones in a small circle.

As you begin hunting for dry twigs to use as tinder, you realize that making a fire will be more difficult than you imagined. You've never actually started a fire before—not on your own, anyway. Mama or Pa always helped get the spark going.

You pat one of your pockets. Your matches are still there! You thought they'd be floating at the  bottom of the river with the catfish. Digging into your pocket, you feel your small knife. This will be very helpful in the future.

With the land and trees still damp from the heavy storm, it takes you a long time to find partially dry kindling. When you finally have a small bundle in your arms, you set it down in the middle of your rocky nook.

Your stomach grumbles. You crave the fatty
bacon, dried meat, and coffee from your family's
wagon. You can already hear Mama laughing at Pa's
silly jokes, and Snap barking after a nearby jackrabbit.
At this point, you'd even be happy to see your aimless
wagon train captain, Buck.

You pull out your matchbox
and stare down in horror. It
popped open while you were
carried away by the river. The few matches you have
left are soaked through, except for one partially dry
match. You'll have to find another way to make a
fire—and you've never made one with steel and flint
before. You can use your small knife as steel. But you
can't find any flint stone.

You keep the wet matches just in case. Maybe you
can use them once they dry out.

Then, you remember a trick one of the wagon
train folks used when they had trouble getting the
campfire started with wet tinder. You rush over to a
small grove of pine trees and take out your knife. You

notch a hole until, slowly but surely, you see resin—
a thick sap—seeping out. It's highly flammable. This
trick is perfect for a time like this.

In your circle of stones, you've laid out the only
dry moss you could find and small kindling wood. You
coat the end of a long stick in the resin and try your
luck on the driest match you have. When you strike
the match, the spark ignites the resin and it flares to
life. You set it among the twigs and gently blow to
help start a flame while you add slightly
larger sticks. In a few minutes, you've got
a small but steady fire going. Relieved,
you start to warm from the heat.

Your stomach's growl interrupts your brief moment of peace. It's been at least a few days since you ate anything. Should you go look for food nearby or construct a shelter for the night?

To make a shelter, turn to page **76**

To find food, turn to page **44**

You keep your distance. You can't be too careful. "I'll get help up ahead!"

After traveling on horseback for a few days, taking shelter in the trees at night, you finally arrive in Oregon City. You feel a mix of relief and melancholy. You should have come into the city with your parents. What if they're not here? What if all of your hopes have been for nothing?

You remember the sick family and head straight for a doctor. The doctor shakes his head but grabs his medical bag all the same, hurrying for his horse.

"Measles." He mounts his horse. "A deadly sickness that's plagued a number of people here in the area. You were right to stay far away—it's highly contagious. You would have contracted it if you'd gotten too close. Thank you for telling me."

The doctor rushes off—you're glad you could help.

As you walk with Snap and your horse through the hustle and bustle of the city, you ponder the impossibility of tracking down your parents.

You're about to head into the general store to buy a bite to eat. Then you hear a familiar voice.

You turn and force yourself to blink—you can't believe your own eyes. "Mama? Pa?"

Your parents whirl around and rush toward you, with tears in their eyes. Snap wags his tail and bounds with joy.

"You're alive!" Mama sobs. "How is this possible? How are you here?"

"We kept searching for you." Pa wipes his eyes. "We looked up and down the river, during the storm. After a week, we couldn't find you. Buck pressed us hard. We had to go on. I've regretted the decision ever since—until today."

Mama wipes her eyes and shakes her head. "We were so frightened."

"Buck just wouldn't listen." Pa puts his hands on

Oregon City
AUGUST 16, 1849

his hips. "He told us that if we wanted to stay behind any longer, we'd be jeopardizing the others. We'd have to stay behind on our own. No wagons. No food . . ."

"We shouldn't have trusted that old fool!" Ma steps in.

You realize that you were both scrambling to find one another in the vast mountain country. Remorse fills your heart, but as you think of everything you've experienced over the past few months with Tatsa, you don't regret anything at all.

You hug them both tightly. "It's all right, Mama, Pa. I'm all right. See? Snap and I took care of each other. We made it!"

Mama kisses Snap on the nose and scratches his ears. "You good boy, you! You protected our child."

"And . . . I wasn't alone, Mama. Not entirely."

"You found another wagon train?" Pa tilts his head.

"Not exactly. I had a friend, Tatsa. The best friend in the world. She saved my life more than once. She's the reason I'm here."

"Where is your friend now?" Mama asks gently.

You smile. "Tatsa is back with her family at a trading post not far from here. She told me that I'd find you again. And she was right."

Mama hugs you once more. "Well, now that we have you back with us, we'll get settled in and build our house. I'd like to go visit Tatsa and her family, to thank them."

"First." You grin. "I'd really love a piece of apple pie, Mama."

"First." Mama grins back. "You're going to need a bath!"

You all laugh. Relief sweeps through you. You can't wait to help Mama and Pa build your new house in Oregon City. And you can't wait to tell them all about your adventures with Tatsa out in the wild.

 **THE END**

GUIDE
to the Trail

It's 1849, and you are making a historic journey West as one of 400,000 adventurous and daring pioneers. You have walked with your wagon train for about 1,000 miles (1,600 kilometers) along the Oregon Trail. You'll have to rely on your survival skills, make friends, and trust your judgment to make it the rest of the way to Oregon City. You will scavenge for food, learn how to make a shelter, and avoid deadly animals. Danger and adventure await you on the Oregon Trail, pioneer!

DANGERS!

 SICKNESS

Cholera, dysentery, and even measles are deadly diseases on the Trail. Dysentery and cholera can come from drinking unclean water or eating uncooked or rotten food. Make sure your food is fresh, and cook it thoroughly. Boil drinking water. Check to make sure your water source is running clean, free of mud and grime. If you come across sick pioneers, keep your distance and try to get help from a doctor.

BAD WEATHER

Be prepared. You will be passing through many different climates. Sudden hailstorms, avalanches, thunderstorms, and bad weather can be fatal. Take shelter in a secure, sturdy location during storms. Make a shelter to protect yourself.

STARVATION

The wilderness is full of natural food sources if you know where to look. Be sure to watch surrounding animals to see what berries and plants they feed from: that's a sign they're probably safe for humans to eat, too. Flowers such as dandelions and rock cress are wonderful snacks in a pinch, and even cattails can be eaten.

FROSTBITE

If you experience frostbite, make sure to wrap the affected area in loose bandages. Do not expose to direct heat, such as fire, which can result in burns and infection. Warm up the damaged skin gradually so as not to cause shock to your system. Do not massage or rub. Be sure to get help if you can.

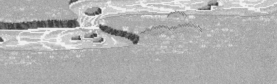

DEHYDRATION

If you're lost in the wilderness, one of the most important things is to find clean water. Set up shelter near a water source each night. If you find a stream or brook, check to see if other animals or people are also drinking from it. If the water looks or smells odd, it may be contaminated. Avoid desert-like areas where water is scarce.

SHELTER

Finding shelter is the most important thing you can do when facing nightfall in the wilderness. You need it for protection and for warmth, and to keep your campfire from blowing out. Build a lean-to by collecting large sticks and lining them up against a sturdy tree. Food, even water, can come later.

ANIMALS

Predators such as wolves can hurt or kill you. Be cautious approaching strange sounds. If you run into a pack of wolves, make yourself big and face them down—do not run away. Don't show your fear. Be careful of mother animals protecting their babies—animals who sense a threat will attack. Always stay alert and be aware of your surroundings.

☞ FINDING YOUR WAY

Try and secure a map. Without one, you have nothing to guide you over the Continental Divide to Oregon City. You don't have a compass—only the sun and stars. Ask for guidance whenever you can. Make wise choices about whom to trust, and stick with experienced travelers. Often indigenous Nations, such as the Shoshone, can provide helpful advice.

Look for landmarks listed here in the Trail Guide.

AGAIDIKA SHOSHONE VILLAGE [LEMHI VALLEY]

This pleasant valley surrounded by the Bitterroot Mountains is home to the Agaidika Shoshone, a nomadic Native American Nation who fish from the nearby Salmon River.

THREE ISLAND CROSSING

This is a crossing along Snake River. Stay to the north of the river, as the south can lead you into the desert and the Bruneau Dunes, where water is scarce.

MOUNT HOOD

The great peak in the Cascade mountain range, Mount Hood provides a long and difficult trek through the Barlow Tollgate.

Look for these landmarks between Missouri and Oregon City:

DISTANCE FROM INDEPENDENCE, MISSOURI:

SOUTH PASS: 914 miles (1,471 km)

AGAIDIKA SHOSHONE VILLAGE (LEMHI VALLEY): 1,260 miles (2,030 km)

THREE ISLAND CROSSING: 1,409 miles (2,268 km)

MOUNT HOOD: 1,720 miles (2,770 km)

The Oregon Trail

LIVE the Adventure!

Do you have what it takes to make it all the way to Oregon City?

Look straight into the face of danger and dysentery.

Read all the books in this new choose-your-own-trail series!

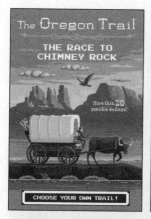

The Oregon Trail

THE RACE TO CHIMNEY ROCK

More than 20 possible endings!

CHOOSE YOUR OWN TRAIL!

The Oregon Trail

DANGER AT THE HAUNTED GATE

More than 20 possible endings!

CHOOSE YOUR OWN TRAIL!

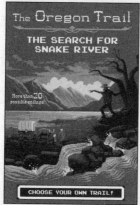

The Oregon Trail

THE SEARCH FOR SNAKE RIVER

More than 20 possible endings!

CHOOSE YOUR OWN TRAIL!

The Oregon Trail

THE ROAD TO OREGON CITY

More than 20 possible endings!

CHOOSE YOUR OWN TRAIL!

The Oregon Trail

THE WAGON TRAIN TREK

More than 20 possible endings!

CHOOSE YOUR OWN TRAIL!

The Oregon Trail

ALONE IN THE WILD

More than 20 possible endings!

CHOOSE YOUR OWN TRAIL!